Hilda

Patsy

bus driver

Teacher

friends

pencil case

ruler

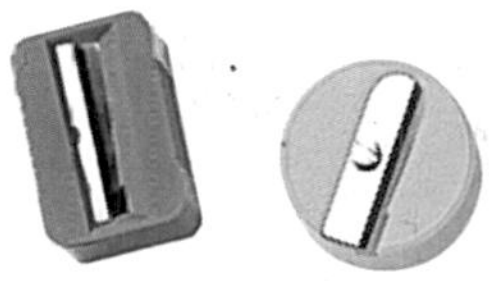
pencil sharpeners

rubbers

crayons

ducks

traffic light

notebook

easel

paints

rectangle

squares

house

Goldilocks

bears

bed

eyes

sandwich

apples

sandcastle

pyjamas

picture

P. B. Bear

A Dorling Kindersley Book

Senior Art Editor Chris Fraser
Art Editor Claire Jones
Project Editor Caryn Jenner
Production Louise Barratt
Photography Dave King

First published in Great Britain in 1996
by Dorling Kindersley Limited,
9 Henrietta Street, London WC2E 8PS
Visit us on the World Wide Web at
http://www.dk.com

Reprinted 1997

A CIP catalogue record for this book is available from the British Library.

ISBN 0-7513-7040-1

Colour reproduction by Colourscan, Singapore
Printed and bound in Italy by L.E.G.O.

Acknowledgments
Dorling Kindersley would like to thank the following manufacturers for permission to photograph copyright material:
Ty Inc. for "Toffee" the dog and "Freddie" the frog
The Manhattan Toy Company Ltd for "Antique Rabbit"
Folkmanis Inc. for "Furry Folk" hen puppet
D.S. Nicholass Limited for the toy pig
Althans KG. for the Althans Club koala bear and penguin

Dorling Kindersley would also like to thank the following people for their help in producing this book:
Barbara Owen, Robert Fraser, Stephen Raw, Fiona Munro, Natascha Biebow, Vera Jones, Alice and Edward Nash

Can you find the little bear
in each scene?

P.B. BEAR'S

SCHOOL DAY

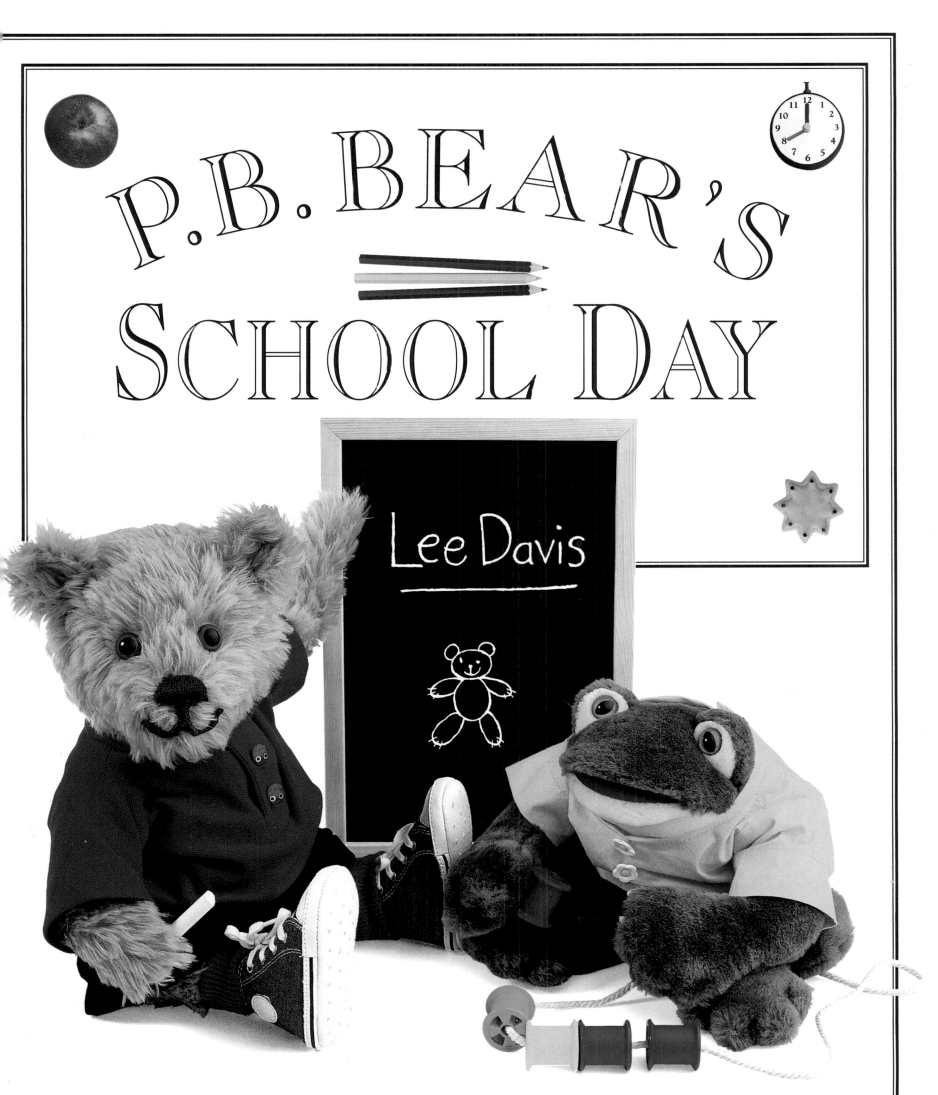

DK
DORLING KINDERSLEY
LONDON · NEW YORK · STUTTGART · MOSCOW

Brrring! went the  . Wake up!

Quickly, P.B. Bear  jumped out of 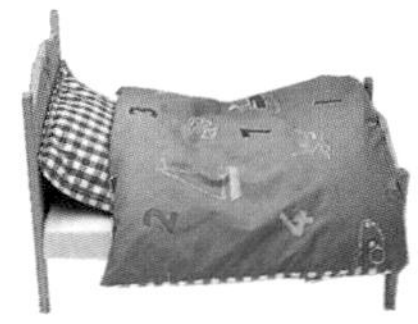 and put on his  and  . Then he found his  and his  . In his  , he put 1  , 2 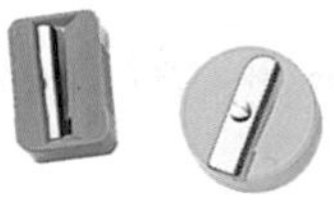 , 3  , 4 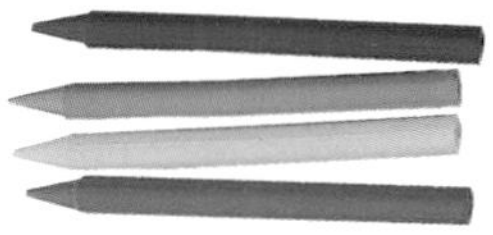 and 5  . Then he put his  into his  and ran out the 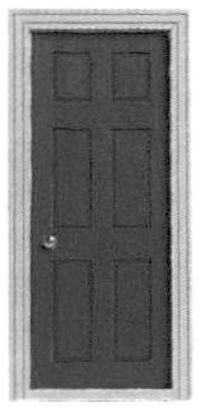 .

Oh dear!  hurried back. He'd nearly forgotten his  .

Now he was ready for school!

P.B.Bear
P.B.Bear

and his friend, Dermott, rode the

they called to the as they drove past. At the next BUS STOP, Hilda and Patsy

shouted, "Go!" "Here we are," said the

when they arrived at school.

BUS STOP
Can you count how many of us ride on the bus?

to school. Florrie and Russell were waiting at the next . "Quack! Quack!"

got on the . The was . "Stop!" called . The turned , and

 and his  went into the school.

Teacher  smiled at them and said good morning.

“Good morning!” called  . He liked  .

 took his  and a  from

his 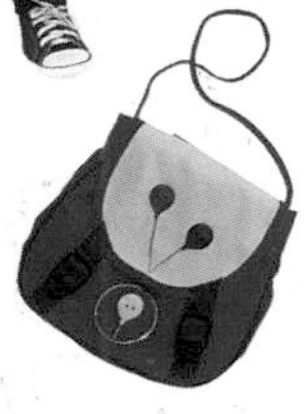 . He wrote his name very carefully

in his 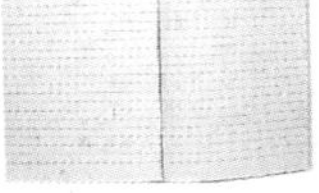 : P and B for P.B. Bear.

What else begins with a P or a B ?

What things begin with the first letter

of your name?

P.B.Bear

 set up the  and  .

 put on his painting  and found his 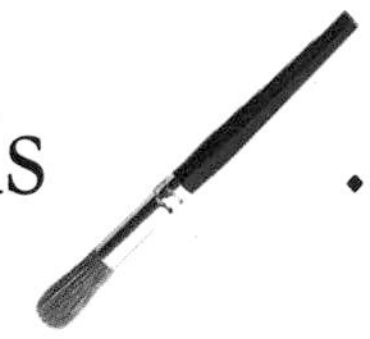 .

He shared the  with  and 
and  . What a mess!

First,  painted a . Then he painted a 
with a  on top . Inside the  , he painted
1  and 2 little  . It was a  !

What colour  did  use?

"It's storytime," said  .

She began to read the story of  and the 3  .

All of the  joined in for their favourite part.

When the 3  arrived home,

Father  said, "Who's been sitting in my  ?"

Mother  said, "Who's been eating my  ?"

Baby  said, "Who is sleeping in my  ?"

All 3  looked in the  .

Goldilocks  opened her .

"Oh dear!" she said.

At lunchtime,  sat outside with his . He opened his . It was packed full!  ate his , then took 2 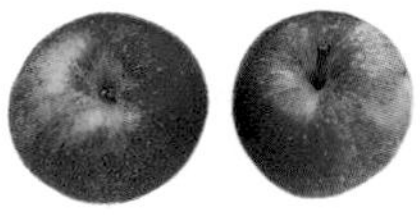 from his . He gave 1  to .

How many apples did  have left?

 had 2 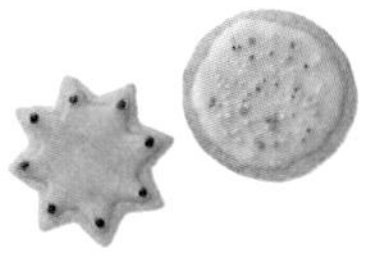 in his 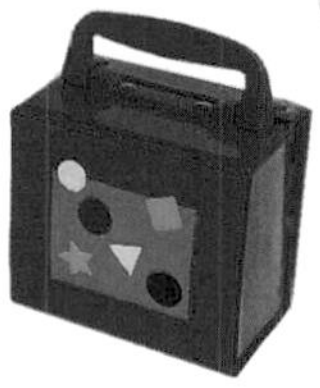 .

Then  gave him 2 more  .

How many biscuits did  have then?

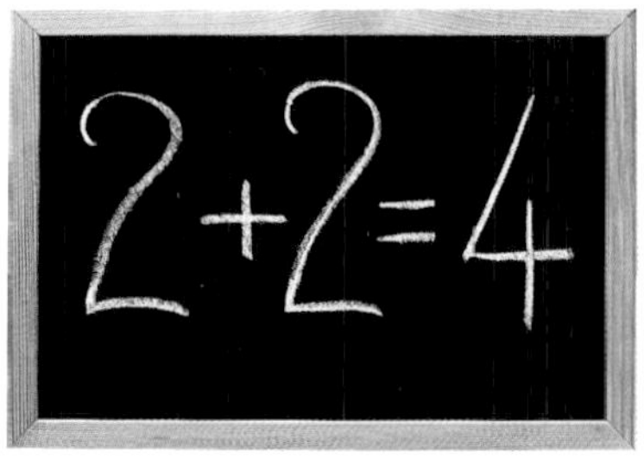

 had eaten his  , his  ,

his  , and his  .

Now his  was empty!

After lunch,  and his  played until the  came to take them home again.

Who is at the top?
Who is down?
Who is at the bottom?

Who is up?

Whose  is **big**?

Whose  is little?

Soon, it was time to go home.

Goodbye, . See you tomorrow!

That night,  was very sleepy. He'd had a busy day at school! He took his  out of his . Then he put on his  and climbed into . Soon, he was smiling in his sleep.

Sweet dreams, !

1ST
PRIZE

P. B. Bear

Dermott

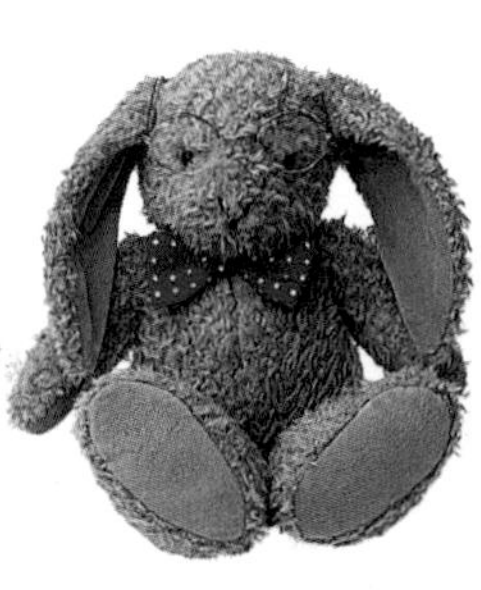

Russell

Florrie

alarm clock

bed

trousers

shirt

satchel

pencils

door

lunch box

bus

bus stop

smock

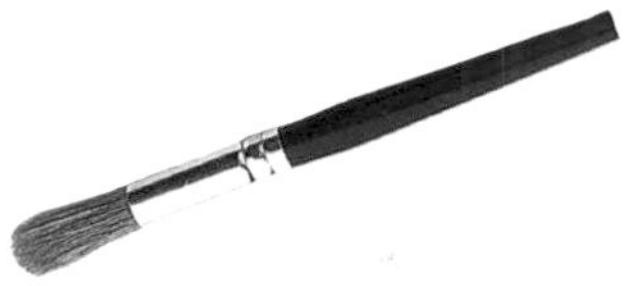

paintbrush

circle

square

triangle

Father Bear

Mother Bear

Baby Bear

chair

porridge

biscuits

lunch box

cake

yoghurt